TO: Ciara & Christian
From: Princess
Speedy
Baller

Note for Librarians: A cataloguing record for this book is available from Library and Archives Canada at www.collectionscanada.ca/amicus/index-e.html
ISBN 1-4120-7412-6

Printed in Victoria, BC, Canada. Printed on paper with minimum 30% recycled fibre. Trafford's print shop runs on "green energy" from solar, wind and other environmentally-friendly power sources.

Offices in Canada, USA, Ireland and UK
This book was published *on-demand* in cooperation with Trafford Publishing. On-demand publishing is a unique process and service of making a book available for retail sale to the public taking advantage of on-demand manufacturing and Internet marketing. On-demand publishing includes promotions, retail sales, manufacturing, order fulfilment, accounting and collecting royalties on behalf of the author.

Book sales for North America and international:
Trafford Publishing, 6E–2333 Government St.,
Victoria, BC V8T 4P4 CANADA
phone 250 383 6864 (toll-free 1 888 232 4444)
fax 250 383 6804; email to orders@trafford.com
Book sales in Europe:
Trafford Publishing (UK) Limited, 9 Park End Street, 2nd Floor
Oxford, UK OX1 1HH UNITED KINGDOM
phone 44 (0)1865 722 113 (local rate 0845 230 9601)
facsimile 44 (0)1865 722 868; info.uk@trafford.com
Order online at:
trafford.com/05-2307

10 9 8 7 6 5 4 3 2

Summer Dreams

When the summer began, we decided to write a book. We wanted to write about something that all kids would like. At first, we could not decide what to write about, so we asked our dad for some advice. Our dad always has a lot of great ideas.

"Every morning when you wake up, write a short sentence about your dreams," Dad said. "After one week of writing down your dreams, write a book about your *best* dreams."

We took Dad's advice and wrote this book. We titled it Summer Dreams.

WHO WE ARE

The Princess: My pen name is The Princess. I am the baby sister of our family. My family calls me Princess, because that is what I am.

Speedy: My pen name is Speedy. I was born before my sister, and after my brother. I love to run. I can run faster than most of the kids I know.

Baller: My pen name is Baller. I am the big brother of our family. My nickname is Baller because I love playing basketball. I once beat my dad in a game of basketball.

Say Cheese
By The Princess

I did it! I passed to the first grade! I knew I would because I made good grades all through the school year. My last report card of the year was the best one of the whole school year. Since I did so well, my parents gave me ten dollars to spend on anything I wanted to buy. I already had five dollars from saving my allowance, so then I had fifteen dollars. My dad took me to the toy store. I bought a Barbie camera that takes real pictures. This summer I took a lot of neat pictures.

I took a picture of my brothers running a race in our back yard. It was a very close race. My brother Baller thought he won the race. My brother Speedy thought the race was a tie. When I got the pictures developed, you could see that Speedy was correct. In the picture, they both crossed the finish line at the same time.

I also took a picture of a beautiful sunset. My family and I were at the park when the sun was going down. The sky was orange in some areas and red in other areas. It was very pretty. It looked like someone had colored the sky with crayons.

I snapped my favorite picture at my grandparents house. I took a picture of a beautiful butterfly. It was a pretty yellow color. It had bright red dots on its wings. It had dark purple lines down the middle of its back. Its wings looked soft and silky. I had forgotten how beautiful the butterfly was, until I got the pictures developed. Later that night, I dreamed about the pretty butterfly.

In my dream, I was laying in a big grassy field. I was looking up at the beautiful blue sky. I was surrounded by colorful flowers that grew in the pretty green grass. The flowers smelled just like candy. I daydreamed about being queen of my own little country, just like the great African Queens my dad tells me about from a long long time ago. As I turned over to lay on my stomach, I saw the most beautiful flower I had ever seen in my life. I plucked the flower and put it to my nose. I wanted to see what it smelled like. Then, the beautiful flower turned into a colorful butterfly. It looked like the butterfly I had taken a picture of in real life. The butterfly leaped to my nose. I giggled because it tickled me.

When the butterfly flew from my nose, I thought it was going to fly away.

Instead, it flew to my ear and spoke in a quiet whisper.

"My name is Lyla. What is your name?" the butterfly said.

I was amazed that the butterfly could talk.

"Everyone calls me Princess," I said.

Lyla flew back to my ear again and said, "Nice to meet you Princess. Would you like to go on an adventure with me?"

I was so excited that I jumped into the air.

"I would love to go on an adventure with you!" I shouted.

Then, Lyla flew above my head. She flapped her wings really fast. When she stopped flapping her wings, I felt wings of my own growing on my back.

"You will need those so you can fly with me," Lyla said.

I flapped my wings and I lifted into the air. Then, Lyla flapped her wings really fast again. When she stopped, my new camera appeared in my hands.

"Bring that along for our adventure," Lyla said.

The first place we flew to was far far away. As we flew through the air, Lyla flew in front of me. She flew near my ear so I could hear her when she spoke.

"If you like the color pink, you're going to love our first stop," Lyla said.

"I love pink," I told Lyla. "It's my favorite color."

Just as I finished my sentence, we arrived at a beautiful place. It was totally covered in pink. Pink trees with pink leaves stood taller than gigantic buildings. A pink river flowed along side of a huge pink mountain. The grass was pink also. Beautiful pink flowers were all throughout the pink grass.

"Wow, this is awesome!" I said. I took a picture of the beautiful pink wonderland.

"Princess, take a look at that pink waterfall over there," Lyla said.

I couldn't believe how pretty the waterfall was. It flowed really fast. It sparkled like it was magic. I took a picture of it.

"Well Princess, we don't have much time. I have two more places I want to show you," Lyla said.

I wasn't ready to leave, because this place was so beautiful. I wished I could stay there forever.

DRAW A PICTURE OF THE PINK LAND

"Can't we stay just a little while longer?" I said.

"Well, we could, but we might not have enough time to see the other places I want to show you. You will be waking up soon," Lyla said. Then she said, "Trust me Princess, the best is yet to come."

After I took one more picture of the pink wonderland, I said, "Okay, I'm ready to go now."

As we flew away from the beautiful pink place, I thought to myself, *This is the greatest place ever.* But when we arrived at our second stop, I changed my mind.

"CANDY!" I shouted as loud as I had ever shouted in my life.

"I thought you would like this place. It's called Candyland," Lyla said.

Chocolate! Caramel! Cotton Candy! Gummi Worms! Peppermints! (Well, I'm not that crazy about peppermints.) Gum Drops! Jelly Beans! Fudge! Taffy! Candy Corns! Candy Apples! It was all there!

I was so excited that I almost dropped my camera. The streets were made of butterscotch. The houses were made of gingerbread. The street lights were made of candy canes. Everything there was made out of candy!

"Would you care for a treat, Princess?" Lyla said.

I quickly said yes. Then I flew down to a candy corn field. It was full of chocolate-covered flowers. First, I ate one of the chocolate-covered flowers. When I plucked the flower from the field, another one grew back in its place.

"Wow, neat!" I said. Next, I ate a handful of candy corns that grew in the field instead of grass. Lyla had flown over to a little pond of honey. She was sipping from it. I took a picture of her. Next, I ate a candy apple and a candy

DRAW A PICTURE OF LYLA AND THE PRINCESS IN CANDYLAND

necklace made out of sweet tarts.

When I was too full to eat another bite, I laid back onto a bed of marshmallows.

"I wish we could stay here forever," I said.

Lyla bounced around in front of me. Then, she flew to my ear and whispered, "This place is nice, but I have somewhere extra special I would like to take you."

Lyla seemed more excited about our next stop than she was about the pink town and Candy Land.

"I'm ready if you are," I told her.

On our way to the special place that Lyla wanted to show me, we flew much higher in the sky than we had flown the other times.

"Let's go up higher," Lyla kept saying.

Each time we went higher, Lyla wanted to go even higher. We went so high that the sky turned dark way up there. The stars came out and began to twinkle. It looked so beautiful up there I wondered if we were in heaven.

"Is this what you wanted to show me, Lyla?" I said.

"No," Lyla said. "What I wanted to show you is straight ahead."

Up far ahead of us, I saw a shiny planet. It seemed to sparkle with different colored lights. I took a picture of the planet as we moved closer to it. Then I heard the sound of a lot of people mumbling. I could not tell what they were saying.

"What is this place?" I said.

Lyla's wings started flapping faster than I had ever seen them move before. The closer we got to the planet, the more excited she became. She kept bouncing around in the air. When Lyla said, "This is my home," I could finally tell what the mumbling voices were saying. I could also see who was mumbling.

"Welcome home Lyla," all the beautiful butterflies said together.

Their whispers combined together sounded like one loud voice. I looked around and I could not believe my eyes. Butterflies were everywhere. They were all different colors and sizes. They were so beautiful.

"We always welcome our visitors with a kiss," Lyla said.

Then, Lyla kissed me on the cheek. Next, a pretty red butterfly with yellow wings flew up and kissed me on the cheek. Then, a blue butterfly, a purple butterfly, and a pink butterfly came and kissed me. The blue one and the purple one kissed my cheeks. The pink one kissed my nose. Then, all of the butterflies started kissing me all at the same time. It tickled so much that I could not stop laughing. Then I heard one of the butterflies say, "Princess, it is time to wake up."

I kept laughing as more butterflies tickled me with their kisses. Then I heard the voice again. This time the voice sounded familiar.

"Mommy's little princess, it is time to wake up."

When my eyes popped open, my mommy was waking me up. She was tickling my nose with a feather.

THE END

My Adventure With Sonic
By Speedy

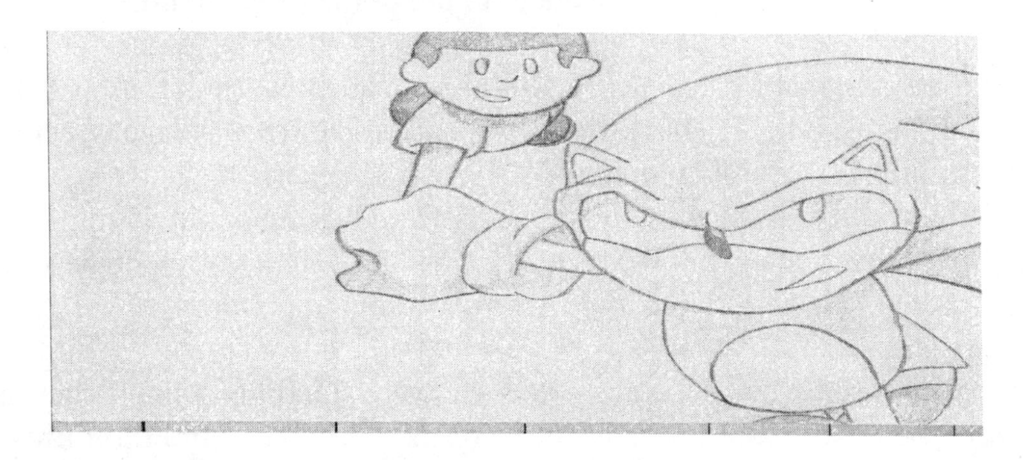

Have you ever had a dream that seemed so real that when you woke up, you felt like it really happened? That's how I felt when I had a dream about Sonic. This dream was filled with a lot of bright lights and colors. I was in a big city that had gigantic buildings. It reminded me of pictures I've seen of New York City. It was night time, but because of all the lighted buildings and cars, it wasn't dark. It was cool outside, but not cold. The cool breeze felt good.

I felt a little strange at first because I was alone. There was a lot of neat stuff going on though, so being alone wasn't too bad. A clown was on a street corner juggling a bunch of colored balls. He was throwing the balls up very high. They would disappear in the night sky for a minute before coming back down. Then I saw a man with the face of a Cheetah. He was across the street from the clown. He was giving away free ice cream to children.

A long line of kids as far as the eye could see were standing in line to get their free share of the ice cream. I wanted some of the ice cream, but I didn't want to wait in such a long line. I started walking away. Then I heard someone yell.

"Hey Speedy!"

When I looked back, the kid in front of the ice cream line was waving at me. He was about the same height as me, maybe a little taller. He was chunky too. He looked like he had already eaten a few bowls of free ice cream. He had dark brown skin. He was almost the same complexion as my big brother. I didn't recognize the kid. I went over to see what he wanted.

"How do you know me?" I asked him.

He smiled and answered with excitement.

"Everyone knows you Speedy! You're a legend!"

That's when I knew I had to be dreaming. I know I'm popular, but I'm not that popular. When I asked the kid what his name was, he told me Luke was his name. Then he asked me if I wanted to get in line in front of him. Of course I said yes.

The Cheetah filled a huge ice cream cone with 20 different flavors of delicious ice cream. The cone was longer than my arm! After I took the first lick from my ice cream mountain, I thanked Luke for letting me get in front of him. Then, right after he said, 'Anything for you Speedy,', I heard loud roaring engines coming down the carnival-like road ***(vrooooom)***. When I turned around to see what was making the roaring sounds, I saw two kids on shiny motorcycles coming in our direction.

One of the kids was riding a red and blue bike. It had the word CYBER written on it. He was wearing a matching red and blue helmet. The other kid was riding a silver and gold bike. It had the words GOLD SPEED written on it. He wore a shiny silver and red helmet. They were riding very fast when they passed us. They made a big gush of wind whirl around us. It almost knocked over my ice cream. When they sped past us, I could see their names on the back of their shirts. The kid riding the red and blue bike was named Wave. The other kid's name was Slider. They appeared to be racing.

DRAW A PICTURE OF WAVE AND SLIDER ON THEIR BIKES

As they approached the end of the road, I could see that there was a cliff in front of them.

"Look out!" I shouted to them.

I wasn't sure if they knew the cliff was ahead of them.

"It's ok," Luke said. "They do this all the time."

I had a confused look on my face.

"Their bikes can fly," Luke said.

Then, Slider's bike lifted into the air, just like in the movie E.T. But then something must have went wrong with Wave's bike. He went off of the cliff and disappeared. That's when I dropped my ice cream cone and took off in the direction of the cliff. I was running faster than I had ever ran in my life. I was moving so fast that everything was a blur. In less than four seconds, I arrived at the edge of the cliff. When I stopped suddenly at the edge, I felt a very strong wind fly by me.

"I got this one Speedy!" I heard a voice say from the wind. "Oh yeah, here is your ice cream cone. I caught it before it hit the ground," the voice said.

Before I had a chance to stand up straight and try to figure out who or what the voice was, Wave was rescued and was back up where I was standing. He was rescued by one of my favorite video game characters by the name of Sonic. Sonic was blue and yellow just like in the video game. He was wearing white gloves and white boots. His ears were pointy.

All the kids in the area gathered around us and cheered.

"Sonic and Speedy! Sonic and Speedy!"

Then Sonic looked and me and winked his eye.

"You're pretty fast kid," Sonic said. "You can get the next one."

Then Sonic's watch started beeping.

"What's that Sonic?" I asked him.

"That's my rescue watch," Sonic said. "It beeps whenever someone needs rescuing. Follow me!" he said.

Sonic sped away so fast that I could barely see him up ahead. I took off and quickly caught up to him. This time I ran even faster than before. My legs were moving so fast that it looked like I had wheels on my feet. While we were running I asked Sonic who were we going to rescue.

"Jack and Terry need our help!" he said.

In just a few short minutes we arrived on top of a hill. The hill was above a big grassy field. Somehow it was now daylight. Jack and Terry looked like they were about my age. They were surrounded by a pack of wolves. The wolves were slowly circling the scared boys like they were ready to attack them. The bigger boy had a big stick in his hand. Sonic yelled to him, "Jack, behind you!" Jack spun around quickly and swung the stick just in time. The stick hit the wolf on the side of its head. The wolf growled ***(grrrrrrrrr).*** The wolves seemed to get angrier then. Terry, the smaller kid, began crying as the wolf pack started closing in.

Then Sonic looked at me and said, "I've got a plan." When he said that, two of the wolves looked our way and growled ***(grrrrrrrrr).***

"I'll distract the wolves by running in a circle around them," Sonic said. "Then you dash in and rescue Jack and Terry and bring them up here."

It sounded like a risky plan, but I was confident that it would work.

"Let's do it!" I said.

Then, just like we planned, Sonic sped away and started circling the wolves. He was moving so fast that pieces of grass were flying into the air. The wolves were trying to bite Sonic, but he was too fast for them.

"Ok Speedy, come rescue the boys!" Sonic yelled.

I could barely see Jack and Terry anymore. Dust was surrounding them as Sonic seemed to be moving faster and faster. Before I headed toward the danger zone down on the field, I bent down and held my head low like a track runner. Then, I took off!

In just a few seconds, I made it from the tall hill to the dusty circle where all the action was going on. I grabbed Terry first. On my way out of the circle, I bumped into one of the wolves. I heard his teeth snap at me as I dashed out of his reach.

I took Terry up on top of the hill where I was before. Then I quickly turned back around to go rescue Jack. When I scooped Jack up, one of the wolves snapped at me. It bit off a piece of my shirt, but I kept moving. By the time I made it back on top of the hill where Terry was, Sonic had left the dangerous circle and joined us.

We looked back down to the field. The dust was starting to settle. The wolves had stopped circling. Some of them were hunched over and were breathing heavily. The other ones were lying in the field. They all looked worn out. Terry had stopped crying since he wasn't in danger anymore. Then, a bus load of campers came by. The driver yelled and pointed our way.

"There they are!" the driver said.

When everyone got off of the bus, Jack explained what happened. Then the crowd of campers started cheering.

"Sonic and Speedy! Sonic and Speedy!"

Terry's mom gave me a big hug.

"Thank you so much Speedy," she said.

Then everyone got back on the bus. I could see tears of joy in the eyes of Terry's mom. It made me feel good to help Jack and Terry. I always enjoy helping others.

As the bus drove away, Sonic and I started walking.

"You did a great job back there, Speedy," Sonic said.

"Thanks," I said. "I've never done anything like that before." Then I asked him, "So where are we going now?"

"Let's go to my house so I can give you a rescue watch," he answered.

I couldn't believe it! Sonic was actually going to give me my very own rescue watch!

"Ok cool!" I said. I was very excited!

On our way to Sonic's house, we started off running, but somehow we arrived at his house on bicycles. His house was painted blue and white. It was huge! It sat high off of the ground. We had to jump from the ground to a set of stairs. The stairs led to his front porch. Inside his house were a bunch of trophies, swords, and video games. He also had a metal punching bag. I was amazed at all the cool stuff he had.

DRAW A PICTURE OF SPEEDY INSIDE SONIC'S HOUSE

As I was looking through his collection of video games, Sonic said, "Hey Speedy, think fast." He tossed me a shiny silver watch. It had a bunch of buttons and lights on it.

"Wow!" I said. I pushed the different buttons on the watch to see what they were for.

Then, Sonic's watch started beeping. We looked at each other. Then my watch started beeping.

Then Sonic said, "Someone needs our…"

Before Sonic could finish his sentence, I was waking up from the sound of my alarm clock. It sounded just like the beeping watch in my dream.

THE END

Everybody Listen Up
By Baller

Have you ever discovered something interesting about your parents that really surprised you? That is how I felt when I discovered that my dad use to rap when he was younger.

One Saturday, my dad and I were cleaning out the garage. We were going through some old boxes and throwing away junk we did not need. One of the boxes we went through had a lot of cassette tapes in it. I didn't know what cassette tapes were until my dad told me. Dad said, "This is what we use to listen to before CD's were invented."

I nodded my head, then I started to count the tapes. That old dusty box had forty-five tapes in it. Most of the tapes were rap tapes. Some of the rappers I recognized were LL Cool J, The Fresh Prince, Run DMC, and Ice Cube. Some of the ones I didn't recognize were The Fat Boys, Two Live Crew, Curtis Blow, and Whodini. My dad told me that the Whodini tape was one of his favorite ones. Dad put the Whodini tape into an old tape player. We listened to it while I kept looking through his old tape collection.

In the bottom of the box of tapes, I found one that had Flex and Kev written on it.

“Who is this group?” I asked Dad.

Dad smiled as if I had found some gold or a buried treasure.

“Let me see that,” Dad said.

I handed it to him and I could tell that the tape was special to him.

“I had forgotten all about this old tape,” Dad said.

“What’s on the tape?” I asked.

Dad smiled at me, but he did not say a word. He took the Whodini tape out of the tape player and put the mystery tape into it. When he pressed the play button, the drum machine and keyboard sounded good. I started moving my head back and forth. Then, a young boy’s voice came on and started rapping. The kid sounded good.

DRAW A PICTURE OF BALLER LISTENING TO HIS DAD'S TAPE

"Do you recognize that voice?" Dad said.

When I heard Dad ask the question while the kid on the tape rapped along with the music, I immediately knew the young voice was Dad.

"Hey that's you!" I said.

The voice on the tape player sounded younger, but I knew it was Dad.

"Yes. That's your old dad," Dad said.

Then Dad started rapping along with the song. I could not believe my eyes or my ears.

Wow, look at Dad! I thought to myself. *He is really good!*

I ran to get my brother and sister so they could see and hear it for themselves. My sister laughed when she went into the garage. My brother danced and tried to rap along with Dad. When my mom walked in, she started laughing. We all started laughing and dancing. Then I went to get my keyboard, because good music always makes me want to play my keyboard. The keyboard is my favorite instrument. I have played it since I was two years old.

When I turned it on in the garage, I turned the volume up as loud as it could go. I pretended like we were a family band performing at a concert. It was a lot of fun.

Later that night, my brother and I talked about how much fun we had in the garage. While we were laying in bed, he said, “Baller, Dad is really good at rapping, isn’t he?”

“He sure is Speedy,” I said. Then I drifted to sleep.

What is this place? I thought to myself.

I was in dream land when the darkness slowly started turning to daylight. This place didn't have any trees or grass. The ground was covered with dirt. The wind blew dust into the air. I heard an explosion in the distance. (BOOM) It was loud like the cannon that blasts at a FAMU football game when the rattlers score a touchdown. Then I saw some army tanks coming my way. Next, I heard gun shots coming from behind me. (POP POP POP POP) I turned around and saw soldiers running toward the tank. They were shooting at the tanks.

This must be a war! I thought to myself. Then, I saw war planes flying in the sky. They were shooting at the soldiers running on the ground.

"STOP!" I shouted as loud as I could. My voice echoed loudly.

It was as if I had shouted into a microphone. Everything stopped. The tanks stopped moving. The soldiers stopped running. The bullet sounds also stopped. Everyone was looking at me like I had something important to say. I stood there quietly. I remembered the words from one of my dad's rap songs. He had rapped about peace and love in one of his songs. I used my own words and I rapped to the soldiers:

War is wrong and it needs to stop.
Before the whole world explodes into tiny rocks.
Killing is evil and makes everyone mad.
A lot of mothers and fathers are really sad.
Because their sons and daughters have died for nothing.
Let's stop the war and stand for something.
Because the world is strong when everyone's together.
And the world will be peaceful forever.

When I finished my rap, the soldiers put down their guns. They walked over to each other and shook hands. Then they came over to me and shook my hand. Everyone was glad the war was over. The soldiers and I went to different villages. We spread the news about the war being over. I rapped in one of the villages:

The war is over. No more worries.
Come outside and hear my story.
You kids don't have to be scared anymore.
No more fallen soldiers in the war.
Today is a new day for the world.
Spread peace and love, boys and girls.
America, Russia, Africa, Japan.
Spread this word as fast as you can.

People slowly started coming out of their homes. They were so happy about the good news. A celebration began in the street. It was like a festival going on. Then, my dream turned dark again.

At first, it was quiet. But then I heard a voice say, "And now, introducing one of the greatest keyboard players in the world. Put your hands together for the one and only, Baller!"

The lights came on and I could see a big room full of people. Everyone was clapping and saying my name. *Baller, Baller, Baller, Baller!*

I was standing on a stage in front of the big room. I looked toward the middle of the stage and saw a big black keyboard. When the clapping quieted down, I began walking toward the keyboard. Then the clapping started again.

When I sat down at the keyboard, the clapping stopped. All eyes were on me. I started playing a slow song I made when I was nine years old. When I closed my eyes, my fingers moved like magic across the keys. I always close my eyes when I play my keyboard at home. Then I heard a voice singing along with the music that I played. I opened my eyes and I saw one of my favorite singers, Usher Raymond, singing:

This is for the mothers in the crowd.
Especially the ones that make me feel proud.
For all that you do to make me strong.
And for teaching us the difference between right and wrong.
To all of the fathers, I'm glad you're here.
Because you make a difference when you're near.
You are always there when we need you.
You take good care of us, this is true.

Everyone clapped as I played the piano and Usher sang the song. When we finished that song, Usher looked at me and said, "It's your turn to get up here, Baller."

Usher tossed me the microphone. I caught it with two fingers. Then I heard the music from one of my dad's songs coming from the speakers. I looked into the audience and I saw Dad. I smiled at him, then I rapped his song:

DRAW A PICTURE OF BALLER RAPPING TO THE CROWD

Just give me a while, it won't take long.
I know I'll have a lot of number one songs.
I'll put my mind to it and give a lot of effort.
You'll be in record bar buying my records.
I don't boast and brag, and don't brag and boast.
But I'm the hottest rapper on the east coast.
I'm one of the two, and together we're a deuce.
Now get out on the floor and let's get loose.

Everyone in the audience cheered my name. *Baller, Baller, Baller, Baller!* Then, the sound of the crowd started fading away. All of a sudden, I heard two familiar voices shouting my name. *Baller, Baller, Baller!* I opened my eyes. My brother and sister were standing over me.

THE END

Magic Fish
by Baller

One Saturday afternoon, my family and I went to the pet store to buy some pet fish. One of my dad's friends had given us a fish tank so I was excited about filling it with new fish. My mom told my sister, my brother, and I that we could each pick out two fish for our new fish tank. My sister was the first one to pick out her fish. The first fish she chose was yellow with a long black tail. She named her Goldie. The other fish she chose was bright pink, which is her favorite color. She named that fish Cindy.

When it was my brothers turn to pick out his fish, he closed his eyes and spun around once while holding out his index finger. When he opened his eyes he said, "I'll take these two right here." He selected two fish that had blue and red stripes down their backs. The fish looked like twin fish. He named them Knuckles and Tails.

Next, I began looking for the perfect fish for me to take home. I wanted to make sure I picked out the two most incredible fish in the entire pet store. The pet store clerk had already scooped out the fish my brother and sister had chosen. Now everyone was waiting for me to make my selections.

As I looked through a large round-shaped fish tank with colorful rocks at the bottom, the pet store clerk asked me, "Would you like for me to scoop a couple of those out for you buddy?"

I thought about it for a second, then I answered, "No. I don't think I want any of these."

I told him that I wanted the coolest fish in the entire pet store. Then he told me, "Don't worry, I'll help you pick the perfect fish." Then he asked me, "So what's your name?"

I told him my name was Baller. Then he asked me what my favorite colors were.

"Red and black, like the Miami Heat baby!" I was imitating my favorite basketball player, Dwayne Wade when I answered him. I pretended like I was dribbling a basketball when I answered. Then, I shot a make-believe basket into the air.

Then, the pet store clerk, whose name was Max, asked me to follow him. He took me to a small fish tank that I had not seen earlier. It was so small that it was easy to overlook. It had some neat looking castles and knights in it. I didn't notice any fish in the tank at first.

"Where are the fish?" I asked Max.

"Take another look," Max said.

I leaned a little closer to the small fish tank. I could see two little fish. These were the most beautiful fish I had ever seen. They were red and black. They swam around together making the same movements. I could tell that there was something special about these two fish. I wasn't sure what it was though.

"I'll take them," I told Max.

"Nice selection," Max said. "These are my two favorite fish in the entire pet store."

Later that night, my little brother played his favorite video game, Sonic. My little sister played with her Barbie doll house. I was in the living room looking at our new fish. I didn't realize that my little sister had come into the living room and was watching me trying to teach my fish how to jump.

"You're wasting your time," she said. "You can't teach fish how to do tricks."

As soon as she had finished her sentence, D-Wade and Shaqy, my new pet fish jumped through the water. They were following the motion of my hand. I looked at my sister and I didn't say a word.

"Awesome!" she said.

Then she came over to the tank and started trying to teach her fish how to jump. Her pink colored fish Cindy just sat there in the water. It looked at her as she tapped on the fish tank. Her other fish Goldie was hiding behind a toy boat the entire time. I'll give it to my sister for being determined though. She kept trying to teach those fish how to jump until it was time for us to go to bed that night.

Before I fell asleep that night, I wondered what other tricks I could teach D-Wade and Shaqy. I thought about them so much that I even dreamed about them that night.

At first, I didn't realize I was dreaming. In my dream, it was a very quiet night in our house. Everyone was asleep. The only thing I could hear was my dad snoring. I decided to get out of bed and check on D-Wade and Shaqy. My little brother and I share a bunk bed, so I was very careful not to wake him. I slowly climbed from the top bunk. I stepped quietly to the living room. I tip-toed over to the fish tank.

When I leaned close to the tank I could see Knuckles and Tails, my brothers fish swimming through one of the toy castles in the tank. They looked like they were playing a game of fish tag. Knuckles was chasing Tails. They were moving super fast. Cindy and Goldie, my sisters two fish, were jumping up in the water. They looked like they were taking turns to see who could jump the highest.

I laughed for a moment before I realized I didn't see D-Wade and Shaqy in the tank. I moved to the side of the tank to look for them. I still didn't see them. Then I became very worried. I went to the kitchen to get a flashlight. When I returned to the fish tank, without even using the flashlight, I could plainly see D-Wade and Shaqy. I scratched my head as I wondered why I didn't see them before. Then, as I was leaning toward the tank, D-Wade and Shaqy disappeared from before me. As I stretched my eyes in confusion, they re-appeared.

"How did they do that?" I whispered. "Could they be magic?"

When I had finished my sentence, D-Wade and Shaqy swam up and down as if they were nodding "yes" to answer me.

I smiled a big grin, then I decided to test my little buddies.

"If you're magic, then make me invisible," I said.

When I said that, the water in the fish tank began bubbling. D-Wade and Shaqy swam up and down. When they stopped moving, I noticed my image slowly disappearing from the reflection in the glass tank.

"Wow, they are magic!" I said with a huge grin on my face.

My dad must have heard me because he came into the living room and said, "Baller, are you in here?"

I kept quiet. I didn't want him to know that I was invisible. When Dad went back to bed I looked back into the tank.

"Can you talk?" I asked my fish.

D-Wade and Shaqy both blew bubbles in the water. The bubbles formed together and spelled the word, NO.

Then I asked them, "What other neat things can you do?"

They blew bubbles again and this time the bubbles formed the words ANYTHING YOU WANT US TO DO.

Now I was really getting very excited. I had my very own magic fish that could do anything I asked them to do! Then I had an idea.

DRAW A PICTURE OF BALLER TALKING TO D-WADE AND SHAQY

"I wish I could walk through walls," I said to my magic fish.

Just then, the water began bubbling again. D-wade and Shaqy swam up and down. I stood in front of the wall leading into the bedroom that my brother and I share. I reached my hand forward to touch the wall. My hand went through the wall. I was amazed! I pulled my hand back, then I walked forward. Before I realized it, I was on the other side of the wall in our bedroom. I was so excited that I started laughing.

"This is so cool!" I said.

Then I heard my mom marching down the hall toward my bedroom.

"Baller, what are you doing in there?" I heard my mom say.

I panicked because I didn't want my mom to come into my room since I was still invisible. I quickly jumped into the top bunk. I pulled the covers over my head. When my mom came into the bedroom, I pretended like I was snoring. I was extremely nervous.

Please don't pull the covers back. I thought to myself.

Then I heard her walk over toward me. My heart started beating super fast.

"Mommy's big boy," Mom said. She rubbed on my back. When I heard her walk away, I was so relieved. I let out a huge sigh.

When I was confident that the coast was clear, I pulled my covers back. I slowly climbed back out of bed. I could hear my brother mumbling something about Sonic in his dream as I quietly stepped down the bunk bed ladder. I walked back through the wall, and into the living room. D-Wade and Shaqy were blowing bubbles. The bubbles formed the words THAT WAS CLOSE.

"It sure was," I whispered to my little buddies. Then I asked them to make me visible again, and they did.

For the next few minutes, I sat in front of the tank watching all the fish playing together. D-Wade, Shaqy, Cindy, Goldie, Tails, and Knuckles swam around chasing each other and jumping through the water. They were having the greatest time. Then, I had a great idea.

"I wish I could swim in the tank with you fish," I said, wondering if this wish could actually happen.

Just like when I had made the other two wishes, D-Wade and Shaqy blew bubbles in the water. They swam up and down. Within seconds, I was inside the fish tank. D-Wade swam over to me and said, "You're it!" He tagged me with his fish fin and quickly sped away.

I looked around the gigantic tank with a huge grin on my face. I could see all the other fish laughing and swimming away from me. It was so exciting being among the fish in their tank. All the toys in the tank looked real. The toy ship was huge. The toy treasure chest and castles were huge also. The light inside the tank made the rocks at the bottom sparkle like glitter. I wanted that moment to last forever. Then I heard Shaqy shout, "Well, what are you waiting for, you're it!"

"Not for long!" I said.

Since Shaqy was the closest fish to me, I swam after him first. I tried to tag him with my new fish fins. I quickly swam after him. I followed him between two plastic bushes. I saw Cindy hiding behind one of the bushes. I swooped down with lightning speed and tagged Cindy on the back.

"You're it!" I shouted.

I swam away from her as quickly as I could. She chased after me for only a couple of seconds. Then she chased after Goldie.

This was the most fun I had ever had in my life, even though it was only a dream. After playing tag for an extremely long time, I began getting tired. I could tell that my new fish friends were getting tired also. Everyone was moving around lazily. I watched as Shaqy swam over to the castle.

"I'm tired guys," Shaqy said. "I'm going in for a nap."

Everyone agreed that taking a nap was a good idea. Chasing each other around in the water had made us very tired. We all followed Shaqy inside the castle and laid down for a nap.

After a few minutes of sleep, I heard a familiar voice saying, "Baller wake up. Wake up!"

Then I felt a small splash of cold water on my face. My dream had ended. I awoke and saw my little brother Speedy sitting on the edge of my bed. He had an empty cup in his hand. I wiped the water from my face and then I said, "Speedy, I'll get you for this!"

My brother jumped from the bed and ran out of the bedroom laughing and shouting.

"Baller thinks he's a fish! Baller thinks he's a fish!" my brother said.

I must have been talking in my sleep again.

THE END

The Hurricane
By Speedy

On our way home from karate practice one day, we passed a sign on the side of the road. The sign said 3 DAYS LEFT TO HURRICANE SEASON. The sign made me a little nervous. It reminded me of the summer of 2004.

Summer 2004 was the scariest summer of my life. The state of Florida was hit by four hurricanes that year.

As I read the hurricane sign, I thought to myself, *I hope this summer is not like last summer.*

Later that night on the news, the weather man said that the first tropical storm of the hurricane season was heading toward Florida. He said the tropical storm might turn into a hurricane. I was so scared that I felt like I almost swallowed my tongue.

Before I went to bed that night, my mom told me not to worry. She said everything was going to be just fine. I could not help it though, I kept worrying.

When I fell asleep that night, I dreamed that I was in the back yard playing hide and seek with my brother and sister. I was hiding behind some bushes when the wind started blowing. A limb fell from a tree and almost hit me. My brother came over and asked if I was ok. I told him I was fine.

"Maybe we should go inside guys," my sister said.

"That's a good idea," I said. "It's starting to get dark out here."

As we were walking to the house, my brother said, "It's too early to be this dark."

"Maybe it's about to rain," my sister said.

As soon as she had finished her sentence, it started to rain. We ran to the door and my mom opened it quickly.

"Hurry inside," Mom said.

DRAW SPEEDY, BALLER, AND THE PRINCESS RUNNING INSIDE

My dad was sitting in the living room watching the news when we came inside. The weather man said that Tropical Storm Arlene might turn into a hurricane. He said the storm was going to make landfall in a few hours.

Oh no! I thought to myself.

My brother, my sister, and I looked at each other, but neither of us said anything.

When the news went off, Dad said, "We need to make sure we have enough hurricane supplies."

"I'll make a list Dad," I said.

"Good idea, Speedy," Dad said. "First we'll make a list of everything we should have. Then we'll make sure we have everything on the list."

I took a piece of paper from my notebook and wrote HURRICANE SUPPLIES on it.

"Let's see, we need a flashlight, batteries, water, and canned food," Dad said.

"We need a radio too," my brother said.

"Yes, we sure do, Baller," Dad said. "Can anyone think of anything else we need?"

"How about a first aid kit?" I said.

"Yes. Put that on the list," Dad said.

We also added paper plates, snacks, blankets, pillows, candles, and matches to our hurricane list.

“Now, let’s make sure we have everything on the list,” Dad said.

My brother, my sister, and I followed Dad to the utility room where we kept our supplies last year.

“The list please,” my sister said.

When I asked her what she wanted the list for, she said, “So I can read from the list and you and Baller can see if we have the items in here.”

My brother and I were able to find everything on the list except for some snacks. Last year we had snacks, but we ate them all after hurricane season. Luckily we had some snacks in our kitchen pantry. We added the snacks to our hurricane supplies in the utility room. This is the room that we would go to if the hurricane came to our town.

When we finished getting our supplies together, we went back into the living room. The weather man was back on the television. He named a lot of counties that needed to evacuate their homes. Our county did not have to leave. The weather man said that everyone in our town should put wood over their windows. When the weather man said that, I got scared. My stomach felt like it was bubbling. I looked at my sister and she looked scared also.

"Don't worry. Everything is going to be fine," Mom said. She hugged my sister and I.

As Mom hugged us, the wind started blowing harder. Then, it started getting darker outside. It started raining harder also. A limb fell on top of the roof. Everyone jumped except for Dad.

"I think I'll go board up the windows," Dad said.

"Do you need any help?" my brother said. His voice was shaking, but he was brave.

"Dad, I'll help also, if you need any help," I said. I was scared, but I wanted to be brave like my brother.

"Thanks guys, but I think I can handle it," Dad said. "Stay in here and protect the ladies."

My brother and I looked at each other, then we said to Dad, "Yes sir." I was glad that Dad didn't need our help.

When Dad finished boarding up the windows, I was happy he made it back inside safely. The weather was getting worse. The weather man said the tropical storm was getting closer to land. Everyone sat in the living room very quietly. As we watched the news, we heard tree limbs falling on the roof. The neighbor's car alarm went off. Then, we heard a strong wind snap a tree in half. The snapping sound was really loud.

Next, the electricity in our house went out. My sister snuggled up to Dad. She began trembling. Dad hugged her and said, "It's ok Princess." My sister nodded her head and didn't say a word.

"I'll get the candles," my brother said.

When I see my brother being brave, it makes me want to act brave, so I said, "I'll go with you, Baller."

My brother and I took the flashlight with us as we walked down the dark hallway to the utility room. While we were walking, we heard a loud crash outside. (CRASH) It sounded like a big tree falling on top of a car. Baller and I looked at each other and we kept walking.

Then we heard Dad shout, "Bring the radio back with you, guys!" Dad's voice surprised us. We both jumped, then we smiled at each other.

When we went into the utility room, something slammed up against the boarded up window. The sound was loud. (BOOM) It scared me so bad that my hand was shaking when I reached for the radio. My brother dropped the flashlight, but luckily it did not break. We grabbed the radio and the candles. Then we quickly ran back to the living room.

When Mom lit the first candle, her face looked so pretty with the fire shining on her. She smiled at me and made me feel a little better. Dad turned on the radio and a voice came on. It said that Tropical Storm Arlene had turned into a hurricane. The voice also said that this was going to be the worst hurricane in history. He also said that the winds were causing a lot of damage already, even though the hurricane was not on land yet.

We sat there for a while listening to the radio, then Dad said, "Let's go to the utility room everyone."

Dad carried my sister in his arms as we all walked down the dark hallway. My brother carried the flashlight. I carried the radio. Mom carried the candles.

After Mom put a candle on a table in the utility room, we all sat down on some pillows.

"Who wants to play UNO?" Mom said. I think she was just trying to make everyone feel better. My sister slowly raised her hand. She was still closely snuggled to Dad.

"Princess and I will be on teams," Dad said.

"I'll play," Baller said.

Then I said, "Me too."

We played UNO for a long time. I won most of the games. Playing cards was a good idea because we did not think about the storm that much while we were playing. The only time we paid attention to the sounds outside was when something crashed into our house.

After we played a lot of games of UNO, my sister fell asleep in Dad's arms. Dad laid her down on a big cushion. Mom laid down beside Princess and went to sleep. Baller stayed up for a little while longer, but then he laid down and went to sleep.

"I guess it's just you and me, kid," Dad said.

"I guess so," I said. "Do you want to play checkers?" I asked.

"Sure. Why not," Dad said.

Dad and I played checkers for a long time. I won every game. In real life, Dad always wins in checkers, but in my dreams, I win.

"Well son, I think I'm going to lay down for a while," Dad said. "Maybe you should too."

I was not sleepy, so I said, "I would rather stay up and listen to the radio."

Dad laid down and went to sleep.

I leaned back against a cushion and listened to the radio. The man on the radio said that hurricane Arlene would be on land in one hour. He also said the hurricane was heading straight for our town.

"Oh no," I whispered. "Should I wake everyone?"

I decided not to wake anyone, because I did not want to scare them.

"I wish there was something I could do to stop the hurricane from coming here," I whispered.

"I wish I could go and beat that bad hurricane."

"That's not a bad idea," I whispered.

I would never try anything like this in real life, but since this was only a dream, it was time for me to go on a mission.

I wrote a note on a sheet of paper for my family. The note said:

Dear Family,
I must defeat the hurricane. I am going to stop it before it reaches land.
Speedy

When I opened the front door leading to outside, the wind blew so hard that the door flew open and knocked me back inside the house.

DRAW THE WIND KNOCKING SPEEDY BACK INTO THE HOUSE

"Wow," I whispered. "This is not going to be easy."

I used all of my strength and walked outside. I closed the door behind me, and I was on my way.

I ran through town as fast as I could. It was hard running through the strong wind. The cold rain was splashing on my face. I was the only person outside in the bad weather. The streets were empty.

As I ran, I noticed a big puddle of water ahead of me. I ran as fast as I could and then I jumped over the huge puddle. Once I landed, I ran even faster than before.

I knew I was getting close to the ocean because the wind was getting stronger. The wind began picking up cars and throwing them at me. I moved quickly and dodged each car. Then, I could see the hurricane in the ocean in front of me. When I moved closer to the ocean, I heard a voice come from the hurricane.

"YOU CANNOT DEFEAT ME, SPEEDY!" the hurricane said. It sounded angry, but so was I.

Then, a lighting bolt came from the hurricane. It came straight at me, but I caught it. Next, I heard a loud boom. (BOOM) Then, a lot of small hurricanes began coming onto land. Hurricane Arlene stayed in the ocean.

I took the lighting bolt that was in my hand, and I threw it at the smaller hurricanes. The lighting bolt made the smaller hurricanes disappear. When the smaller hurricanes disappeared, hurricane Arlene spun around faster and started coming onto land.

"GET OUT OF HERE!" I shouted to the hurricane.

I heard laughter come from the hurricane as it moved onto land. Then, I saw a long arm come from the hurricane. The arm tried to grab me, but I was too fast. I picked up a long rope that was near me. I made a lasso with the rope. I began to twirl it around.

"WHAT ARE YOU GOING TO DO WITH THAT?" the hurricane said.

Then, I threw the lasso around the hurricane. The hurricane spun me around and made me dizzy, but I held on tight to the rope. The rain started coming down faster and faster. Lighting bolts were shooting from the sky. More smaller hurricanes began coming out of the ocean. Hurricane Arlene started spinning even faster. I held on as tight as I could.

"LET ME GO, SPEEDY!" hurricane Arlene said.

"NEVER!" I shouted. I held on even tighter.

Then, the hurricane started slowing down. I wondered if it was getting tired from spinning so much. I pulled the lasso and began dragging the hurricane back to the ocean.

When I was close to the ocean, the smaller hurricanes joined hurricane Arlene and it started getting its strength back.

"Oh no," I whispered.

Then, I felt the hurricane trying to spin me around again.

"NO! GET OUT OF HERE!" I shouted as loud as I could.

Then, I spun the lasso as hard as I could. I used all of the energy and power in my body. I let go of the lasso and the hurricane went high up in the sky. When it was higher than an airplane flies, I heard a voice come from the sky.

"I will get you next time, Speedy!" the voice said. Then, the hurricane disappeared.

The sun came out, but it was still raining. I saw a colorful rainbow over the ocean. I closed my eyes and I smiled. I was happy I beat the hurricane. The rain slowed down. Small drops of rain were bouncing against my face. Then, a big splash of water slapped me in the face.

"Speedy, I said wake up!" a voice said.

When I opened my eyes, I said, "Wow, what a dream."

My brother was sitting on the edge of my bed. He had an empty glass in his hand. I had water on my face.

"I told you I was going to get you back," my brother said.

THE END

The Monster's Cave
by The Princess

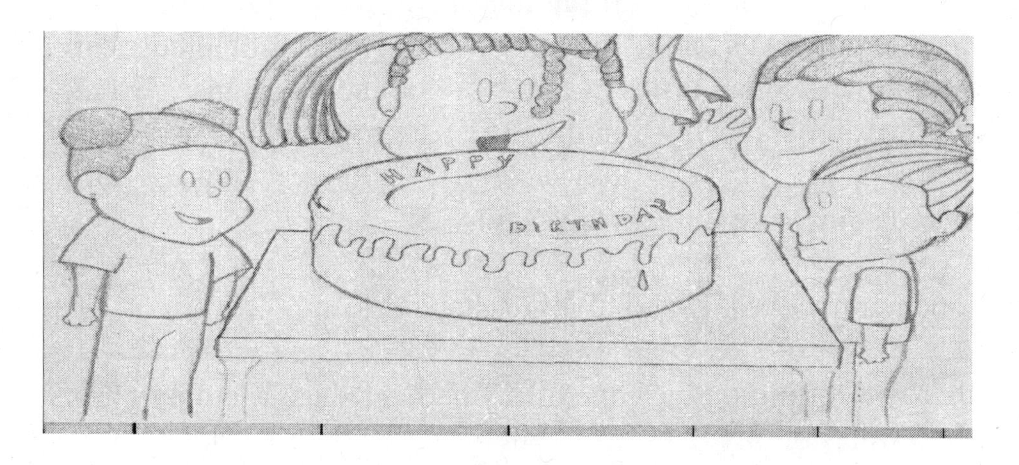

One night I dreamed I went to Gina's house for her birthday party. She is 8 years old. She and I play together on the playground everyday. There were 18 girls at the party. No boys were allowed. We played games and sang happy birthday to Gina. We played so much that I got hot. I needed to cool off, so I went to the refrigerator to get a banana popsicle. Banana is my favorite flavor. I looked and I looked but I didn't find any popsicles, so I closed the refrigerator door. When I closed the door, I was no longer at the party. I was in a dark cave. This place was very scary. I could hear loud stomping. The stomping scared me. I quickly turned around to look for a door. I found a door but it was locked. I yelled for my friends.

"Gina, Suzy, Amy, please help me!" I shouted.

When my friends didn't come to my rescue, I became very sad and more afraid. Then I closed my eyes real tight. I thought something bad was going to happen. But then the loud stomping stopped. I opened my eyes and looked around the big dark cave. I started walking slowly. I wanted to find another way out of the scary place. I peeked around a corner. I saw a messy-looking room with a small lantern sitting on a broken table. Pizza boxes and popsicle wrappers were all over the floor. What I saw next scared me so bad that I wanted to scream. Over beside a big bed of rocks, I saw an ugly, huge, creepy-looking monster. It was sitting in a big black chair with the words Monster Chair written on it. The monster was big! It had green skin and purple hair.

I started backing away to get out of there. I stepped on some of the popsicle wrappers. The sound of the popsicle wrappers made the ugly monster turn around and look in my direction. His eyes were bright blue. His teeth were shiny yellow. He also had a little pink piggy nose.

"Who is here in my cave!" the monster shouted.

When he turned around I thought he saw me, but he didn't.

I slowly started walking away to look for another way out. The more I walked, the darker the cave became. I wanted my daddy so bad that I almost started crying. But I wanted to be a big girl so I didn't cry. After I walked around the dark cave a little while longer, I heard the loud stomping again. Then, you won't believe what happened next. I heard a little voice tell me to face my fears. The voice made me feel better even though the stomping was getting louder. Then I turned around and walked into the direction of the stomping. When I was back to the area where the monster was, I saw why the stomping was so loud. The monster was dancing and jumping around. I listened carefully. I could hear music coming from Gina's birthday party. Then I took a deep breath before I said, "Excuse me. I'm lost."

The monster did not hear me. He kept dancing around and jumping. I took another deep breath, and this time I spoke louder.

"Excuse me, Mr. Monster!" I shouted.

Then the scary-looking monster quickly turned his big head around. His bright blue eyes looked into my eyes. His little pig nose started twitching. I was very afraid. But then the monster said, "Monster, what monster!" Then he ran and tried to hide behind the chair he was sitting in earlier.

DRAW A PICTURE OF THE MONSTER HIDING BEHIND A CHAIR

Doesn't he know he's a monster? I thought to myself.

When I saw his eyes peek from behind the chair at me I was no longer afraid. I could tell that he was more afraid of me than I was afraid of him. I walked closer to the area where he was hiding. I could see him shaking.

"Please don't hurt me," he cried.

His voice was trembling so bad that I began to feel sorry for him.

"I won't hurt you," I told him. "I'm just a little girl."

He peeked at me again and said, "You look like a big girl to me."

Then I became really calm. The monster was correct. I am a big girl because I faced my fears even though I was very afraid.

DRAW A PICTURE OF THE PRINCESS TALKING TO THE MONSTER

"Come on, it's okay," I told him. I wanted him to come out and stop hiding.

I spoke very quietly to try to calm him down, and guess what, it worked! He slowly stood from behind the chair. He was very tall. He was still shaking a little bit. I asked him what his name was. He said he didn't have a name. I asked him if I could just call him monster. He shook his head and answered, "No, I don't like monsters." Then I asked him, "But aren't you a monster?" Then it was quiet for a little while, but then he started laughing.

"I guess I am a monster," he said. Then I started laughing with him.

"But you're a good monster," I said.

The monster and I laughed and talked for a long time. I told him about my brothers and my mom and dad. Then the monster asked me if I wanted a popsicle. When I answered yes, he told me to look inside the refrigerator.

When I opened the refrigerator, I didn't see any popsicles, so I closed it. When the door closed, I was back at Gina's party with all my friends. Then I woke up from my dream.

THE END

DRAW A PICTURE OF YOUR FAVORITE PART OF THE BOOK

ISBN 141207412-6

9 781412 074124